That Bad Rat!

Written by Kathryn Knight
Illustrated by Josh Eacret

LEVEL **PRE 1** READER

READING LEVEL
PRE K – K

Dalmatian Press

Look at that rat.

That rat

BATS

the cat.

That rat

pulls the mat.

That is not a good rat.

Not at all.

Bad, bad rat!

This is not
a happy cat.

The cat
taps the hat.

The cat
pats the hat.

The cat has

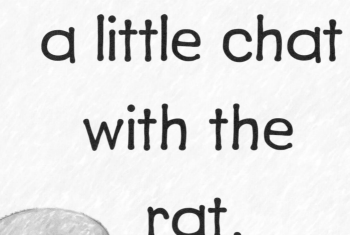

a little chat with the rat.

Now the cat

is fat and happy.

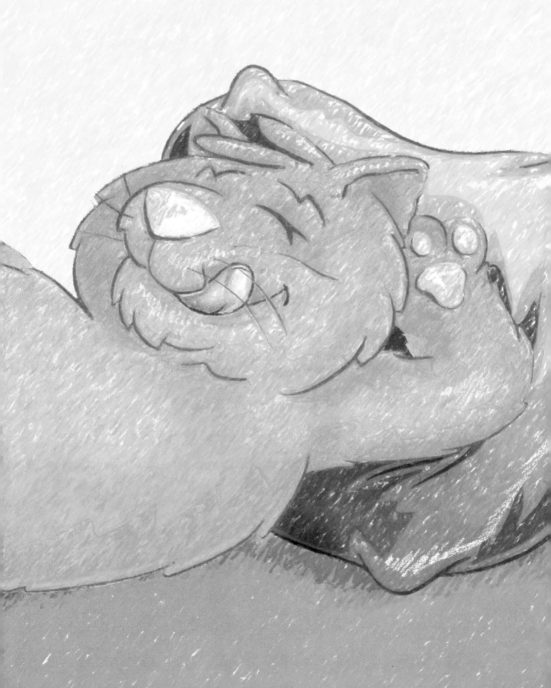

Good, good rat.